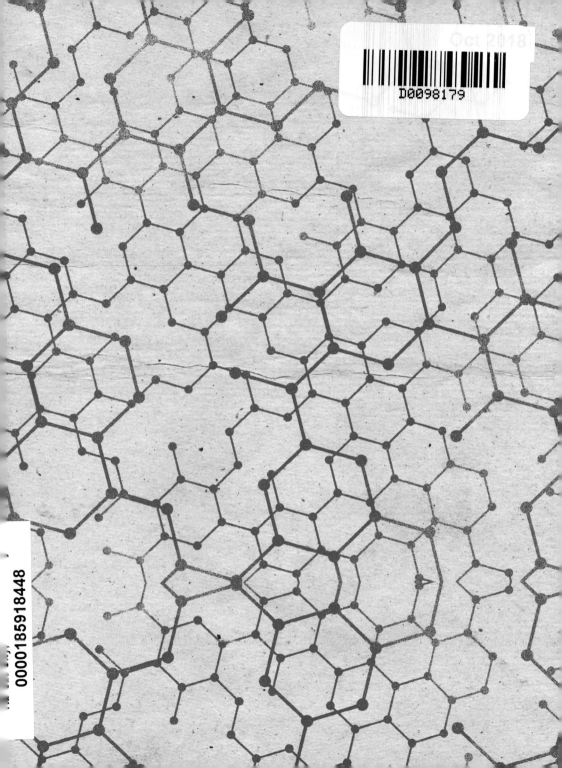

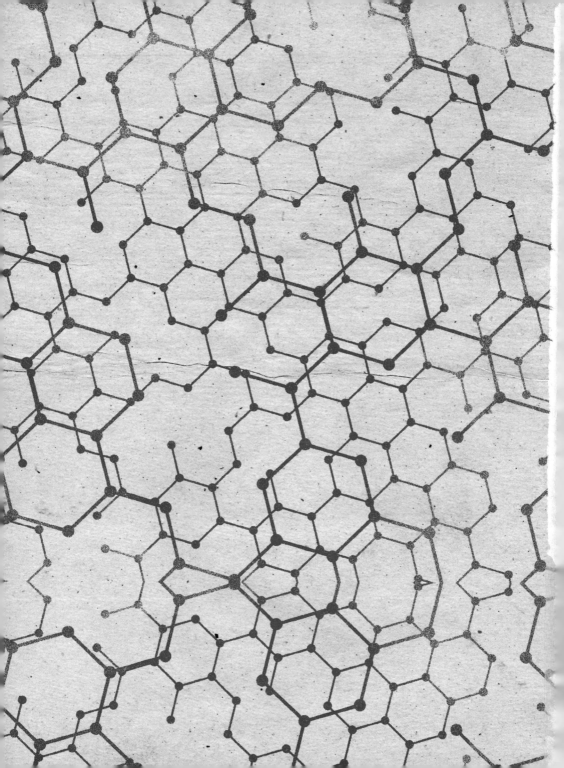

The ACADIA FILES

Book Two, Autumn Science

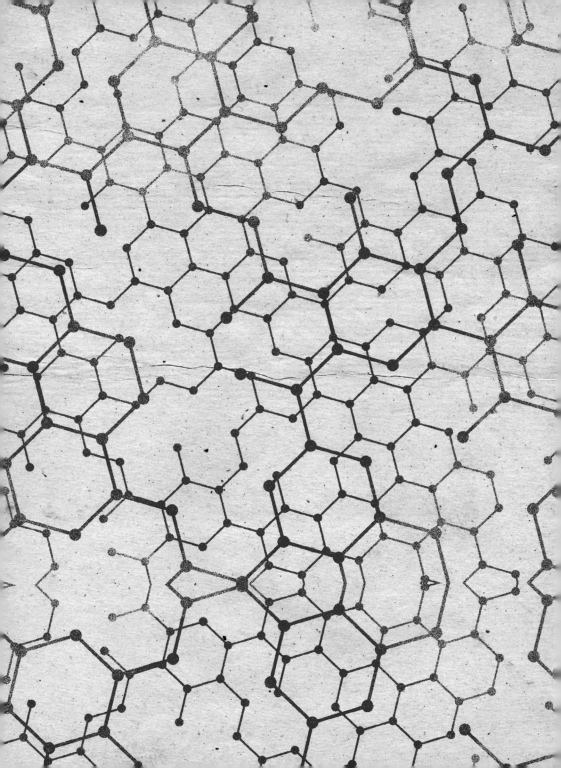

The ACADIA FILES

Book Two, Autumn Science

Katie Coppens

Illustrated and designed by
Holly Hatam

TILBURY HOUSE PUBLISHERS, THOMASTON, MAINE

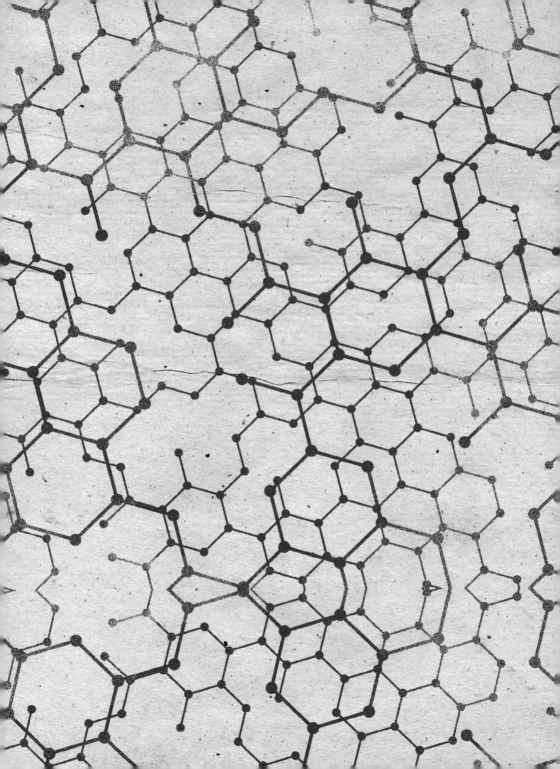

Contents

"Try to make sense of what you see, and wonder about what makes the universe exist. Be curious."

— Stephen Hawking

1
The Frog Pond

One afternoon, Acadia, Isabel, and Acadia's mom are walking Baxter on a forest trail. It's a peaceful fall walk until Baxter's favorite adversary, a bird, swoops down and flies up toward the trees. Baxter pulls so hard when he sees the bird that his leash comes loose from Acadia's hand.

"Baxter! Stop!" Acadia yells.

Baxter soon loses track of the bird, but he keeps running anyway because he smells his second favorite thing: water. Acadia, Isabel, and Acadia's mom chase him through the mix of maple, birch, and oak trees. When they finally catch up, Baxter is neck deep in a mucky green pond filled with cattails and lily pads.

Acadia's mom claps her hands and yells, "Baxter, come here!"

Standing at the edge of the pond, Acadia hollers, "You silly dog. Get over here!"

But Baxter is very happy in the water, and he doesn't seem to hear them.

As Acadia watches Baxter swim away from shore, she notices a frog hopping in the tall grass that fringes the pond. "I think it'll be awhile before Baxter swims back," she says. "Isabel, do you want to help me catch that frog?"

Acadia's mom sits down on the shore and starts to take her shoes off. "Hold on, girls. We don't have a net."

"I don't need a net," Isabel says. "I can catch a frog with my hands."

"I'm sure you can," Acadia's mom answers, rolling up her pant legs. "But you still need a net."

"Why?" Acadia asks.

"Because you shouldn't touch frogs with your bare hands."

Isabel looks down at her hands. "Why not?"

"Because frogs can breathe through their skin. We rubbed ourselves with insect repellent before we left, and the chemicals on your hands could get into the frog."

Acadia says, "That's crazy. Wait, we don't breathe through our skin, right?"

"No," Isabel answers, smiling. "Air goes in our mouths or noses to . . ."

"Our lungs," Acadia nods. "I knew that. So frogs don't have lungs?"

Acadia's mom steps into the mucky water. "Frogs have lungs and breathe in through their nostrils, but they can also take in dissolved oxygen through their skin."

"That's so weird." Acadia looks down at her arm. "Imagine if we breathed in through our skin. Wait, why do we even need air?"

Acadia's mom steps knee-deep into the water and whistles to Baxter. She answers over her shoulder, "Oxygen travels from your lungs to your blood."

"Why exactly?" Acadia asks. Acadia can see the science teacher in her mom excited to talk about this, but she can also tell that her mom is focused on getting Baxter back ashore.

Acadia's mom walks back toward the girls. "Do we need to talk about this right now?"

The girls nod to confirm that, yes, they do need to talk about this now. "Okay. You both know I love it when you're curious. Your arteries deliver blood from your heart to your body. Blood transports oxygen from your lungs to your cells."

"What are cells?" Acadia asks.

"They are often called the building blocks of life. You have trillions of cells in your body that carry out functions. All living things have cells."

Acadia points to the water. "So those lily pads have cells?" Her mom nods. "Does water have cells?" Acadia looks at the pond and thinks about water falling from the sky as rain or coming from the faucet. "Wait, water doesn't have cells because it isn't alive. But it has living things in it like algae and . . . Baxter."

Acadia's mom looks back at the water. "Yes, like Baxter. Okay, girls, let's do this together. Yell 'Baxter, come' on the count of three. One, two, three . . ."

"BAXTER, COME!!!"

Baxter finally obeys and approaches the muddy shore wagging his tail. Acadia grabs Baxter's soaked leash and squirms as Baxter shakes his muddy yellow fur. Acadia squeals, "Baxter! Gross!"

Isabel, Acadia, and Acadia's mom drip with green, mucky water.

Looking at the algae on her arms, Isabel says, "Now I'm really glad that I don't breathe through my skin."

"Me too," Acadia laughs, wiping mud from her cheek.

When Acadia looks again at the pond, she notices bottles floating in the water and a plastic bag caught in the cattails. This is a pond she visits often to see brightly colored dragonflies and hear frogs croaking. She likes to listen to the frogs and imagine what they are talking about, but today all she hears is the wind rustling the leaves of nearby trees. Looking more closely at the water, she sees trash stuck among the cattails. "If frogs breathe through their skin, is pollution extra bad for frogs?"

"It is," Acadia's mom answers.

"Can frogs die if there's too much pollution?" Acadia asks.

"Frogs are vulnerable because they take in toxins through their skin and lay their eggs in water. Because they live in the water *and* on land, scientists study frogs to learn how healthy an ecosystem is. When frogs are healthy, it's an indicator that the air and water are clean. If a frog population is declining, it can mean that their habitat is polluted."

"I think that's happening here," Acadia says. "I've only seen one frog today, and there used to be so many here."

Isabel adds, "You're right. There are way fewer frogs than there used to be."

"I know I can't touch the frogs, but I can pick up the trash." Acadia reaches for a plastic bag that's caught on a cattail and starts to fill it with trash. "Can we come back with a big trash bag and pick up all the litter?"

"Absolutely," Acadia's mom says.

"How do you think all this trash got here?" Isabel asks.

Acadia's mom answers, "It starts with one person leaving a bottle, then someone else does it, and before you know it the pond looks like this."

"I think if they had a trash can somewhere on the trail or next to this pond, that would help," Acadia says.

"I think so too," Isabel says.

Acadia asks, "How can we make that happen? Do you think I could write a letter to the town and tell them about all this trash? We could take pictures of what it looks like and write about what's happening to the frogs. I bet they have no idea that frogs can breathe through their skin and what happens to them when water is polluted. Do you think they'd listen?"

Acadia's mom smiles. "I think they might. And if they don't . . ."

"Then we'll keep saying it until they do," Acadia answers, as she picks up a crushed can off the ground.

Baxter barks sharply and pulls back toward the pond.

"For now, I think the frogs and birds will be happier when we get Baxter out of here," Acadia's mom says.

"Me too," Acadia agrees. She holds the bag of trash in her hand as they head toward the trail. She looks back at the pond, determined to help save it and the frogs that live in it.

Acadia, Isabel, and Acadia's mom return to Rearis Pond two times to collect litter and take photos. Acadia uses this information to write a letter to the town council:

Dear Town Council,

I am writing to request that a trashcan be placed at Rearis Pond. A few weeks ago, I went on a walk there with my mom and a friend and we were horrified by all of the litter. I have gone two times since then and every time there has been trash; we found everything from potato chip bags to a chair in the water (yes, a chair!). I'm including photos of what the pond looked like before and after we cleaned up the litter.

I don't know if you have been to Rearis Pond, but it used to be beautiful. I would hear frogs croaking and see colorful dragonflies. Now, even on a beautiful, warm day, there are hardly any frogs. That is not good. Frogs are indicator species. That means they are an indicator of how healthy an environment is. Because frogs breathe through their skin and lay their soft eggs in water, they are extra vulnerable.

A trashcan could lead to less pollution at Rearis Pond, which is good for frogs and people. I truly believe that one little trashcan could make a big difference.

Thank you for your time and consideration,

Acadia Greene
10-year old
resident

Data From Our Visits to Rearis Pond:

Visit Number	Trash That We Collected
1	* 6 plastic bottles * 4 plastic bags * 4 gum wrappers * 3 bottle caps * 3 aluminum cans * 2 clear ice coffee cups with straws * 1 glass bottle * 1 plastic fork * 1 granola bar wrapper * 1 sandwich bag
2	* 2 plastic bottles * 2 small potato chip bags * 1 little toy car (I think this was left behind by mistake.) * 1 aluminum can
3	* 2 styrofoam cups (one with lid, one without) * 1 plastic bag * 1 straw * 1 plastic bottle * 1 chair (yep!)

Before Clean Up:

After Clean Up:

how did a chair get there?!

Frogs are so cool!!

oxygen in →

oxygen in

lungs

Frog Life Cycle

Adult frog

Eggs

Tadpole

Tadpole with legs

Young frog (Froglet)

NEW SCIENCE WORDS

Environmental Indicator

Something that helps you better understand what is happening in nature. It can be anything from the frog population to the temperature of the water.

Abiotic Factors

The non-living parts of an environment.

sun   wind   rain   water   soil

Biotic Factors

The living parts of an environment.

Trees   plants   bugs   animals

Organism

Any living thing. An organism has cells.

Cells

The building blocks of every organism. They allow life to exist because they help us grow and make up all the systems inside of us.

There can be single-cell organisms

OR

Organisms with trillions of cells

Things I Still Wonder:

- If people see litter already on the ground are they more likely to litter? For some reason, do they think it's okay because other people did it first?

- What would happen to all of this trash at Rearis Pond if no one picked it up?

- What happens to a habitat when there is really, really bad pollution?

2

Why Leaves Change Color

Acadia looks up at the bare branches of the maple tree, then down at the leaves that surround her. The leaves look like a tie-dye collection of colors: red, orange, yellow, green, and brown. She's piling them as high as she can for that glorious moment when she can run and jump into the giant mound and feel the crunchy leaves cushion her fall.

"Can I jump in those?" Joshua asks from his side of the fence.

"I'm going to jump in them when I'm all done," Acadia says as she lifts the rake with one hand and holds the leaves tight to it with the other. She dumps the leaves on top of the pile, but a few get dropped in the process.

Joshua hops the fence and picks up the dropped leaves. "If I help you rake, can I jump in them too?"

"I'm almost done," Acadia says as she rakes a few more leaves to the pile. Then she thinks about how much nicer Joshua has been lately and adds, "But if you promise to help me bag them, you can jump in them after me."

"Good deal." Joshua pushes the leaves together, making the pile extra high.

Just as Acadia sets her rake down, she hears a loud bark from Baxter. He runs through the pile in pursuit of a bird that flies up toward the maple tree.

"Baxter!" Acadia yells.

Baxter gives up on the bird, which is way out of reach, and before Acadia can stop him, he rolls happily in the leaves, scattering the pile.

"Oh, Baxter," Acadia groans.

"I guess Baxter wants to play in the leaves too," Joshua says, then heads into the open garage and grabs another rake.

Acadia is surprised to realize that she's grateful for Joshua's help. He uses his endless energy to gather even more leaves, and before she knows it, the pile is taller than before.

"You first," Acadia says to Joshua.

"Really?"

"Go for it!"

Joshua puts down his rake, takes a running start and jumps into the leaves. He lies there for a second, then leaps up to grab a rake. "Hold on. Let me get the pile really high for you."

Acadia runs and jumps with a huge grin on her face. The leaves scatter around her curly blonde hair, supporting her like a pillow. She lies back with her arms stretched out and smiles up at the blue sky. "I love the fall. Do you think they call it fall because that's when the leaves fall?"

"I don't know. Maybe. Why do the leaves fall?" Joshua asks.

"Now that you're in fourth grade, you'll learn that in school this year," says Acadia, who is in fifth grade. "Trees kind of take a little nap when it's cold. Without leaves, it's easier for them to survive the winter. Trees with broad leaves, like maple or oak, are called deciduous trees. Trees with needles and cones, like pine and spruce, are coniferous trees. Some conifers are called evergreens. Get it, for-*ever green*, because their leaves stay green?"

"Wait. Are needles a type of leaf?" Joshua asks.

"It totally confused me at first too, but they are. The leaves of pine, spruce, and fir are needle-shaped."

"Cool." Joshua holds up an orange-and-yellow maple leaf. "You know a lot. Do you know why this kind of leaf changes color in the fall?"

"Why, yes I do. Like I said, you'll learn this in science class this year, but I'll tell you ahead of time. Then you can act wicked smart in class. The colors, like that bright orange and yellow, are always there, but we only see the green in leaves because of the chlorophyll."

"What's chlor-o-fil?" Joshua asks.

"Chlorophyll is the green stuff in leaves that captures energy from the sun, through light. Sunlight helps plants make food. When there's less sunlight in the fall and the temperature changes, the green chlorophyll fades away. When the green goes away, we can see the other colors that were always there, but hidden."

Joshua holds up a red leaf. "So the color was there the whole time . . . hiding?"

"Well, the green chlorophyll was making it hide. As soon as the color had a chance to come out, we were able to see it."

"I'm kind of like a leaf," Joshua mumbles as he kicks a leaf.

"What do you mean?"

"Sometimes I . . . . Nothing."

Acadia softens her voice. "Joshua, what do you mean?"

"Nothing, I just . . . um . . . you forgot the most important thing about leaves. They're fun to jump in!" Joshua says as he leaps on the pile.

"You got that right!" Acadia jumps on the leaves and sits down beside him.

Joshua picks up a leaf and looks at it. "I can't believe the color was there the whole time."

Acadia thinks about the leaf looking one way to everyone but being different on the inside. She thinks about how much Joshua has changed over the past few months. "Joshua, are you like a leaf because you're nice underneath, but most people don't see it?"

Joshua answers quietly, "Kind of. Most people don't really know me."

"Sometimes I think your mouth is like your adaptation."

"What's an adaptation?"

"It's something that helps plants and animals survive in their environment. Like how birds blend in with trees or fly so fast that Baxter can never catch them."

"Kids pick on me because I'm short. So I say mean things before they start to pick on me. I guess you're right—having a big mouth is how I survive in my environment. Now, nobody picks on me. Of course, nobody really likes me either."

"I do. You're my friend."

"No, I'm not."

"Yes, you are. Just be yourself and people will like you."

Joshua's checks start to turn pink. "Do you want to kick the soccer ball around when we're done bagging the leaves? I'll be the goalie."

"Okay, but you'll need more adaptations than having a big mouth on the soccer field!" Acadia shouts as she takes one final jump in the leaves. She sits up and adds, "In nature, the species with the best adaptations to their environment survive."

"What does that mean?"

"To put it simply, it means I'm going to beat you in soccer."

"We'll see."

"Yes, we will." Acadia smiles at Joshua as he helps bag the leaves.

Later in the day, Acadia keeps thinking about Joshua acting one way on the outside while hiding who he really is on the inside. Acadia goes through the bag of leaves and pulls out a mix of colors. She sorts the leaves by color and makes an art project based on what Joshua said. She takes a photo and adds it to her science notebook.

NEW SCIENCE WORDS

Photosynthesis

The process of plants making sugar. A plant takes in water, carbon dioxide, and sunlight and gives off oxygen.

Chlorophyll
oxygen
Sunlight
water
Carbon dioxide

Chlorophyll

The green stuff in plants that absorbs sunlight.

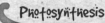

Leaves, Needles, Grass, and algae all have chlorophyll

Producer

Organisms that make their own food (they produce it).

← Flowers and plants make their own food

Consumer

Organisms that rely on other organisms for their food (they consume it). I am a consumer.

Rabbits and sheep are consumers

Things I Still Wonder:

- What causes people to change?

Acadia loves jumping in piles of colorful leaves and dressing up for Halloween, but her absolute favorite thing to do in autumn is playing soccer. Soccer is especially fun this year because Acadia and Isabel are on the same team. They've started a new tradition of having a sleepover the night before a Saturday morning game.

"Acadia, make sure you pack your shin guards," Acadia's mom says.

"And your raincoat," Acadia's dad mutters as he chops oranges for Acadia's soccer team to snack on during the game.

"I hate rain. I bet half our team won't even show up," Acadia mutters.

"They'll show up. This is the playoffs," Isabel says.

Just as Acadia's dad cuts the final orange, the phone rings.

"Hello?" Acadia's mom answers. "Flooded? Oh, no. Isabel's here too. I'll let her parents know. Okay, thanks for calling."

"Please tell me that wasn't what I think it was," Acadia says when her mom hangs up the phone.

"I'm afraid so. That was your coach calling to say that the field is too wet for your game. It's been cancelled. Sorry, girls."

"No! I was finally supposed to start today," Acadia groans.

"I'm sure you'll get to start the next game," Isabel offers.

"What are we going to do now? Rain makes everything so boring."

Acadia's mom sits beside them at the kitchen table. "You can watch a movie or—"

"Is there anything we can do outside?" Acadia asks.

"You have extra rain boots. Why don't you go splash in the puddles?"

"Um, my feet are really big. There's no way I can fit into Acadia's boots," Isabel answers.

"You can wear mine if you'd like. They're right over there." Acadia's mom points to the mudroom off the kitchen.

"Why is it raining so much? It's been raining for two days," Acadia says.

"You want to know something cool about rain?" Acadia's mom asks.

"Wouldn't that be snow?" Acadia's dad interrupts with a big smile. "Sorry, that's a poor attempt at science humor."

"Why is that funny, Dad?"

"Your mom said, 'Want to know something cool about rain?' If it's cold enough, rain becomes snow. Get it?"

"I get it, but why is that funny?" Acadia teases.

"Anyway," Acadia's mom continues, "a cool fact about rain is that it's possible that the rain that's falling right now is the same water that the dinosaurs drank."

"Is that another joke?" Isabel asks. "Your family has a strange sense of humor."

Acadia smiles at Isabel.

"No, it's true," Acadia's mom says.

"But dinosaurs lived a long, long time ago. Hasn't all that water disappeared?" Acadia asks.

"Water doesn't just disappear," Acadia's dad says as he flashes his hands like a magician.

"I think she means, hasn't all that water evaporated," Isabel offers.

"Yes, water does evaporate, but then it comes back down," Acadia's mom says.

Acadia's dad waves his hands. "It's magic."

"Except it's not really magic; it's the water cycle. The water on our planet has been here long before the dinosaurs and will be here far longer than us." Acadia's mom reaches for a pot. "Let's put some water in this pot, and I'll show you." She adds an inch of water from the faucet and places the pot on the stove with the heat turned on high. "The water in the pot could have been anywhere. At one time it could have been inside a dinosaur, or in a tropical ocean, or frozen in a glacier, or flowing down the Nile River. It could have been in Baxter's water bowl, or it could have been . . ."

"Toilet water?" Acadia asks.

"That's so gross. We drink toilet water?" Isabel asks.

"Hear me out. The water on our planet, in whatever form it comes in, recycles itself. A cycle is like a circle. It keeps going and going and going."

"What does that have to do with dinosaur water?" Acadia asks.

"What happens when the water in the pot starts boiling?"

"It bubbles," Acadia answers.

"And does it all stay in the pot?"

Isabel jumps in. "No, the water starts to evaporate."

Acadia's mom smiles. "Exactly! The same is true of the water on our planet."

"But how? The ocean's not boiling," Acadia points out.

"Ocean water still evaporates. In fact, the majority of Earth's water is ocean water, so . . ."

Acadia furrows her eyebrows. "So that means the majority of Earth's evaporated water is from the ocean?"

"Yes! I'm boiling this water to speed up the process, because the warmer the water, the faster it evaporates. But even cold water evaporates. Think about it. If you leave a cup of water outside, eventually that water will disappear. And where did it go? It didn't really disappear; it evaporated."

"I get it!" Isabel says. "Water in a cup that's outside would evaporate faster in the summer than in the fall because it's hotter in the summer."

"Exactly. The water that evaporates becomes water vapor, which is the gas phase of water. Look—see the steam coming off the pot? It's like a cloud. Eventually the vapor builds up in clouds. Then it comes back down."

"As rain or snow," Isabel adds.

"Yes. Then the water droplets will land somewhere, probably in an ocean or a lake or into the grass, and eventually it evaporates back to the sky."

"Then it happens again?" Isabel asks. "And again?"

"Exactly. And the cycle keeps going on and on . . ."

"So the same water that the dinosaurs drank could be in these oranges?" Acadia points to the plate of sliced oranges.

"Yes. That water would have had countless journeys through the water cycle between then and now. Those water droplets could have ended up where oranges grow."

Acadia reaches for an orange and takes a bite. "But now I'm eating it, so isn't the cycle done?"

"Acadia?" Acadia's dad says with a quizzical look. "Can you think about where the liquid from the orange you just ate will go next?"

"Into me," Acadia answers as she chews.

"*And then?*" Isabel giggles.

"Oh, I get it. Gross."

Acadia's mom adds, "But that's not the only way out for the water you take in. Some is breathed out—"

Isabel adds, "Like how you can see your breath in the winter. That's because of the water vapor."

"Yes, exactly. And some comes out as sweat. But most of it is absorbed into your body to help it function. But you're right, Acadia, some of it does end up in the toilet."

"Then where does the toilet water go?" Acadia asks.

Her mom answers, "After you flush, the water is treated. Then it will eventually evaporate again."

"So, wait, the rain that's flooding the soccer field could be the same water that was in our toilet?" Acadia asks.

"Or it could've once been a professional soccer player's sweat," Isabel interrupts. "Isn't that so cool!"

"I guess that is kind of cool," Acadia says.

"Do you want to go play outside?" Isabel asks.

"There you go. Celebrate this rainy day!" Acadia's mom says with a smile.

"Instead of calling it a rainy day, I think we should call it a dinosaur pee day," Acadia says.

"I get it, because the rain could've been . . ." Isabel giggles as she puts rain boots on.

"Or we could call it armpit sweat day? Or sewer shower day? Or . . ."

"Okay, okay, I think you two understand the water cycle now," Acadia's mom says. "I'm going to use this water for tea. Enjoy your time outside."

"Enjoy your dinosaur pee tea!" Acadia says with a smile as she and Isabel run outside giggling.

After Acadia and Isabel come inside, Acadia's mom shows them how they can create their own water-cycle model using water, food coloring, and a plastic bag that zips closed. Acadia makes a model, then comes up with an idea for how she can use it in an experiment.

EXPERIMENT

My question: Will evaporation happen faster in a sunny area or a shady area?

Research: It turns out that the sun's heat is a key part of the water cycle. The sun's heat is essential for evaporation.

Hypothesis: If I put one plastic bag model of the water cycle in a sunny window and another in a shady window, then evaporation will happen quicker in the sunny window because there is more heat.

Procedure:
1. On the top part of the plastic bag (that zips closed) draw some clouds with a permanent marker.
2. Fill the bag with 1-2 inches of water.
3. Add one drop of blue food coloring to the water.
4. Tightly close the bag.
5. Repeat the same process with a second bag (make sure they have the same amount of water... otherwise it's not a fair experiment).
6. Tape one of the bags to a window that gets a lot of sun.

7. Tape the other bag to a window that gets less sun.

8. Observe the bags until you see evaporation happening or for a set amount of time (like 2 days).

Materials: Water, food coloring, permanent marker, and two plastic bags that can zip closed.

Observations:

Water Cycle Model in a Sunny Window	Water Cycle Model in a Shady Window

Conclusion: There wasn't a big difference between the two models. In fact, the one that is in the shadier spot actually showed water evaporation and clinging to the sides first. I think this is because we had our wood stove going and it's in the same room as this model. I think the heat levels in the house messed up the experiment. This experiment would be better to do when the heat in our house is not on, so it's the sun's heat that could (possibly) show a difference.

The water we drank could be the water you drink!

Condensation

Precipitation

Evaporation

The Water Cycle ...water cycles...
again and again
and again
and again...

NEW SCIENCE WORDS

water cycle

The cycle of water moving through Earth's ocean, freshwater, land, plants, animals, and sky.

Condensation

Precipitation

Transpiration

Evaporation

Run off

Percolation

Groundwater

Transpiration

When water leaves plants and evaporates to the air.

It's kind of like plant sweat

Evaporation

When water goes from being a liquid to a gas.

The steam coming off boiling water

Condensation

When water vapor collects.

Condensation

This can form clouds

Precipitation

Rain, snow, sleet, or hail that comes down from clouds in the sky.

Rain   Snow   Sleet   Hail

Things I
Still Wonder:

- How did water first get on Earth?
- How do clouds form? Why are they different shapes?
- How many water molecules are in a cup? A pool? A lake? The oceans? The Earth?

Acadia and her dad are watching game one of the World Series, eager to see what will happen next. Her dad leans toward the TV as the pitcher winds up and throws a fastball straight into the catcher's mitt.

"No!" Acadia's dad hollers at the TV. "Another strikeout! He didn't even swing!"

The camera pans on a sea of blue-and-white jerseys in Dodger Stadium. The crowd noise is deafening. Los Angeles Dodger fans cheer and hold up signs with backward "Ks," showing their pride in another strikeout.

"They'll come back, Dad. The Red Sox always do."

"It's still early in the game, it's still early . . ." Acadia's dad mutters to himself as he looks at the clock. "But Acadia, it's not early in our house. It's nine o'clock—time for bed."

"Dad, I want to stay up and watch the game. It's the World Series!"

"Acadia, it's only the top of the third inning. The game won't end until eleven o'clock or later."

"Why are World Series games on so late? It doesn't make sense. Kids like baseball too."

"It's so everyone across the country can watch the game at the same time," Acadia's dad answers, his eyes on the TV.

"What do you mean?"

"It's nine o'clock here, but it's only six o'clock in California. People there are just getting home from work."

"Wait—so you're saying that right now, at this exact moment, it's two different times? That's crazy."

"Actually, at this exact moment there are way more than two different times showing on clocks around the world."

"What are you talking about?"

"Remember your bear, Bob, and how we talked about how it takes Earth twenty-four hours to make one rotation on its axis?"

"And 365 days to go around the sun."

"Good memory. Think about the bear. Right now it's nighttime for half of the world and daytime for the other half. So the time of day is different depending on where you are in the world."

"I get why we're different than Australia, but why are we different than California?"

"In Maine, we have the first sunrise of anywhere in America. Guess where in Maine you can see the sun first?"

"Where?"

Acadia's dad points to her. "From your namesake."

"Acadia National Park? That's so cool!"

"Yep, from the top of Cadillac Mountain. When the sun comes up in Maine, it's still dark in other parts of the country. As Earth rotates, the sun slowly makes daylight across the states, east to west. Or like right now, it's dark here, but it's still light in part of the country."

Acadia looks at the TV and notices he's right. She can see an orange-pink sunset sky around Dodger Stadium in California, while it's pitch black outside in Maine. "So it's the same moment, but different times. That's so crazy. Hold on—if it's three hours earlier in California, what time is it in Hawaii right now?"

"It's a five- or six-hour difference depending on the time of year, so it's—"

"Kids there might still be in school! I bet kids there are complaining about why the World Series games are on so early. They still have it better than us. They get to see the last few innings of the game instead of the first few. Who even thought of having time zones in the first place?"

"There never used to be time zones at all. People just kind of guessed what time it was by looking at the sun or by clocks in the center of town. Time zones were established in the late 1800s. Can you figure out one of the major reasons why?"

"People didn't know what time it was, so they were always late?"

"Good guess. But something occurred in the late 1800s that made everyone realize there had to be standardized times."

"What are standardized times?"

"Set times."

Acadia thinks about all the things she has to be on time for. "Was it because kids started going to school and they got in trouble if they were late?"

"Another good guess. But think of something that impacted everyone."

"A lot of people went to church. Is that why?"

"Hold on—I don't want to miss this batter."

The word *miss* lingers in Acadia's mind. What is something that she would miss if she had the wrong time? She'd miss a TV show, but there wasn't TV then. She'd miss a plane if she was late, but there weren't planes. There weren't planes, but there were . . . "Trains. It was because of the trains!"

"You got it! Because of the trains, it couldn't be up to just anyone to decide what time it was. Think about it—people would constantly be missing trains. So in the 1880s, when time zones were set, it made everything far more organized."

"It also made it so kids had to go to bed at a certain time, which isn't fair."

"I think kids have always had bedtimes."

"How do they decide exactly where one time zone ends and another begins?"

"It's tricky for states that are right on the border between two time zones. For instance, parts of Indiana are in one time zone and parts of it are in another. So you could leave your house at 5 p.m., drive to the next town over, and find out that it's a little after 4 p.m. there."

"That's so cool. Let's pretend we're in Indiana and it's an hour earlier."

"Hold on, Acadia. Bases are loaded with a full count."

"It's so cool to think about the whole country watching this moment, but at different times—"

"Here's the pitch . . . . Yes! A line drive and . . . yes! A run scored!"

"Can I at least stay up until the end of the inning? It's only fair that I watch until the kids from Hawaii are home from school and able to start watching. It's like we're pinch runners for each other, but instead we're pinch TV watchers."

"I'd hate to let down the kids of Hawaii. You can stay up until the end of the inning, but no more discussions. Let's just enjoy the game. After the third out, bedtime."

"Deal." Acadia looks at the TV and sees the sun setting, then looks out the window at Maine's dark night sky, and is in awe of how amazing the world is.

The next day, Acadia keeps thinking about time zones and how times of sunset can vary according to a city's location. She researches the times of sunset in all the major league baseball teams' cities and makes a data table to show the results.

SUNSET

Data on October 25th Sunset Times:

Team Name	Location of Stadium	Sunset Time on October 25th
Boston Red Sox	Boston, MA	5:47 PM
New York Yankees	New York City, NY	6:01 PM
New York Mets	New York City, NY	6:01 PM
Philadelphia Phillies	Philadelphia, PA	6:07 PM
Baltimore Orioles	Baltimore, MD	6:13 PM
Washington Nationals	Washington, D.C.	6:16 PM
Miami Marlins	Miami, FL	6:44 PM
Tampa Bay Rays	St. Petersburg, FL	6:52 PM
Pittsburgh Pirates	Pittsburgh, PA	6:25 PM
Toronto Blue Jays	Toronto, Ontario	6:18 PM
Cleveland Indians	Cleveland, OH	6:30 PM
Atlanta Braves	Atlanta, GA	6:52 PM
Cincinnati Reds	Cincinnati, OH	6:45 PM
Detroit Tigers	Detroit, MI	6:35 PM
Chicago Cubs	Chicago, IL	5:54 PM
Chicago White Sox	Chicago, IL	5:54 PM
Milwaukee Brewers	Milwaukee, WI	5:53 PM
St. Louis Cardinals	St. Louis, MO	6:09 PM
Minnesota Twins	Minneapolis, MN	6:11 PM
Kansas City Royals	Kansas City, MO	6:26 PM
Houston Astros	Houston, TX	6:40 PM
Texas Rangers	Arlington, TX	6:44 PM
Colorado Rockies	Denver, CO	6:06 PM
Arizona Diamondbacks	Phoenix, AZ	5:42 PM
Seattle Mariners	Seattle, WA	6:03 PM
Los Angeles Dodgers	Los Angeles, CA	6:07 PM
Los Angeles Angels	Anaheim, CA	6:06 PM
San Diego Padres	San Diego, CA	6:04 PM
Oakland Athletics	Oakland, CA	6:18 PM
San Francisco Giants	San Francisco, CA	6:19 PM

OBSERVATIONS OF DATA

* The local time of sunset is almost the same in Seattle as it is in New York because of time zones. In real time the sun goes down over New York three hours before it goes down over Seattle, but Seattle's clocks are set three hours earlier, so it evens out. That's what time zones do!

* HEY, WAIT A MINUTE! Pittsburgh and Philadelphia are in the same time zone, and both cities are in Pennsylvania and at a similar latitude, so why does the sun set 18 minutes later over Pittsburgh? That's because Philadelphia is on the east side of Pennsylvania and Pittsburgh is on the west side, and the sun sets earlier (in real time) over places to the east. But the sun rises earlier over Philadelphia, too, so each city gets about the same amount of daylight.

* WAIT ANOTHER MINUTE! Pittsburgh and Miami, Florida are in the same time zone and on a similar line of longitude (around 80° West), so why does the sun set 19 minutes later over Miami? Oh, I get it: It's because the times of sunrise and sunset depend on latitude as well as longitude. Miami is closer to the equator, so it gets longer daylight on October 25 than Pittsburgh does.

* And why is Arizona so different from other places nearby? It turns out that Arizona doesn't take part in daylight saving time.

24 HOURS TO ROTATE = 24 TIME ZONES?

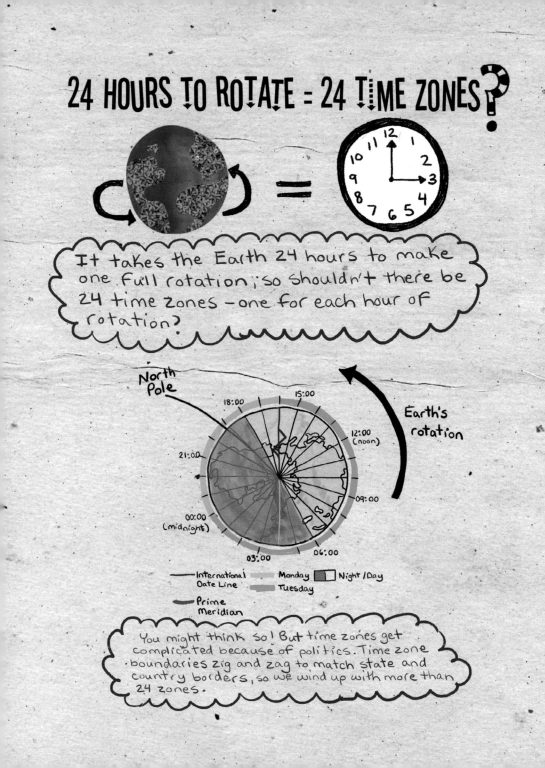

It takes the Earth 24 hours to make one full rotation; so shouldn't there be 24 time zones — one for each hour of rotation?

North Pole

18:00
15:00
12:00 (noon)
09:00
21:00
Earth's rotation
00:00 (midnight)
03:00
06:00

International Date Line
Prime Meridian
Monday
Tuesday
Night/Day

You might think so! But time zones get complicated because of politics. Time zone boundaries zig and zag to match state and country borders, so we wind up with more than 24 zones.

THE U.S. AND CANADA HAVE EIGHT TIME ZONES

Canada

Pacific Time Zone 6:00

Mountain Time Zone 7:00

Central Time Zone 8:00

Eastern Time Zone 9:00

Newfoundland Time Zone

Atlantic Time Zone

Maine

U.S.

Mexico

5:00

Alaskan Time Zone

(Alaska is way bigger than this)

Hawaiian Time Zone
3:00 (2,000 miles west of California)

NEW SCIENCE WORDS

Time Zone

An area of the world that sets their clocks to the same time.

There are ↑ **24** Time zones

more than
(maybe as many as 40!!!
I give up!)

International Date Line

The line that is the official start of a new day. It's near the line of longitude for 180 degrees, but it zigs and zags around islands in the Pacific.

The line is not actually there. It's imaginary.

Greenwich Mean Time (GMT)

It sets the time for all of the world. GMT is the time on the PRIME MERIDIAN, which is the longitude of 0° 0' 0". That's the line of longitude that runs through Greenwich, England (because guys in England invented the system). It's on the opposite side of the world from the International Date Line.

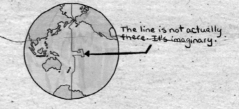

What time is it?

What time is it?

what time is it?

Prime meridian meridians

equator

I know!

Sir GMT

Daylight Saving Time (DST)

In the Spring (March in the U.S. and Canada), when the days get longer, we change our clocks ahead by one hour ("spring" ahead) so that daylight lasts longer into the evening when people are awake and active. In many countries, this is known as "summer time."

7:30PM

Standard Time

In the fall (November in the U.S. and Canada), when the days get shorter, we change our clocks back by one hour ("fall" back) so that it gets lighter earlier when we're heading to school and work in the morning. I learned that more than 60% of the countries in the world use standard time all year round.

7:30 am

SCHOOL BUS

Things I Still Wonder:

- Where did the idea for daylight saving time come from?

- If you tried really hard (with car, train, or plane), in how many different locations on Earth could you celebrate New Year's Eve? So cool to think about 24 hours of New Year's Eve celebrations happening around the world!

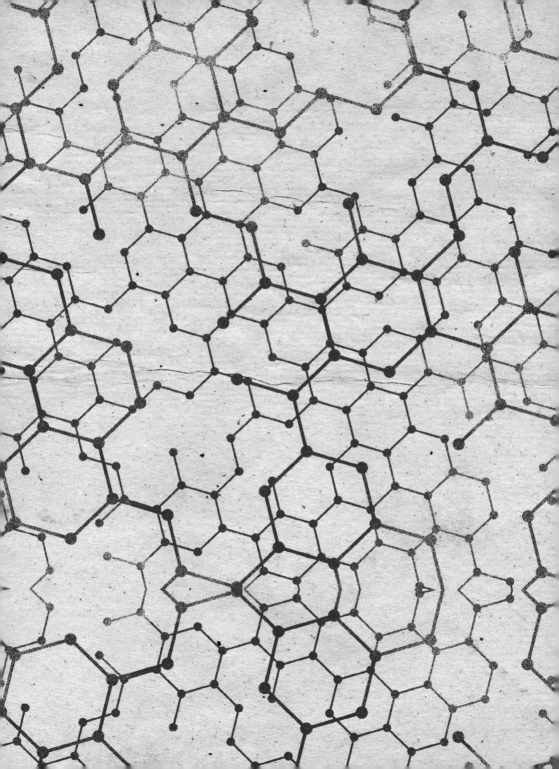

5
The Germ War

After two hours of trick-or-treating, Acadia and Isabel walk into Acadia's kitchen. Each of them is holding a pillowcase full of candy.

"Wow! You made out well," Acadia's mom says while watching the girls plop their heavy pillowcases onto the table.

"I love Halloween," Acadia announces as she unwraps a piece of candy and pops it into her mouth.

"Did people understand your costumes?" Acadia's mom asks.

Isabel answers "Nope," as she stretches out her bat wings.

"Most of the costumes were scary instead of clever. We saw a lot of zombies and ghouls," Acadia adds, as she starts to wipe off her raccoon face paint.

"Nocturnal animals are scary too. You don't want to cross paths with a skunk at night. Baxter and I learned that the hard way," Acadia's mom says.

There is a loud knock at the door, and Acadia's mom answers it with an almost empty candy bowl in her hand. "Oh, hi Joshua. Great costume!"

"Thanks!" Joshua steps into the house dressed up like a giant piece of bacon. Baxter runs over to Joshua and starts sniffing and wagging his tail.

Acadia smiles. "Baxter, he's not real bacon. How was trick-or-treating?"

"Good!" he answers as he lifts a nearly full bag high in the air. "Any chance I can do some candy trades with you?"

"Okay." Acadia turns her pillowcase upside down and dumps colorful, candy-filled wrappers all over the table.

Isabel looks through her bag. "I'll trade with you, too."

Joshua looks at Isabel's wings and long black hair wrapped up and around two pointy black ears. "Isabel, I like your bat costume." Then he looks at Acadia's smudged face paint. "What are you supposed to be?"

Acadia holds up her gray-and-black tail. "I'm a raccoon. Get it? A raccoon and a bat out at night. We're . . ."

"Let me guess—you both have rabies?" Joshua smiles. "Sorry, that was supposed to be a joke."

"Very funny, but no, we're nocturnal animals," Acadia says.

"What's that mean?" Joshua asks.

Isabel jumps in. "They're animals that come out at night. Get it? You trick-or-treat at night."

"Cool. I'm bacon because I *really* like bacon. My dad even found this spray that smells like bacon. Smell." Joshua reaches out his arm to Acadia, then to Isabel.

Isabel smiles. "Now I see why Baxter was confused. You do smell like bacon."

Acadia eats a chocolate bar, then starts organizing her candy. "Back to the candy. Before I trade, I need to sort it into piles. Candy that's my favorite, candy that's okay, my least favorites, and a pile of the peanut butter cups. I give the peanut butter cups to my dad because those are his favorite."

Joshua adds, "I only sort two ways. Candy I can eat and candy I can't eat."

"Why can't you eat some candy?" Isabel asks.

"I'm allergic to peanuts." Joshua pulls out an orange wrapper from his bag and adds it to Acadia's pile. "Here's a peanut butter cup for your dad."

"So you've never had a peanut butter cup? That stinks!" Isabel says.

"I'm kind of used to it." Joshua says. "It could be worse, I could be allergic to bacon," he adds with a smile.

"What happens if you eat peanuts?" Isabel asks.

"It only happened once. That was how we found out I was allergic. My mouth got all red and itchy and my throat got tight and it was hard to breathe."

"That sounds really scary." Acadia holds up a peanut butter cup wrapper. "I don't get it. How can this little piece of candy do that to you?"

"If I eat peanuts, my body thinks there's something really bad inside me and tries to fight it. My doctor said it's kind of like my body thinks the peanuts are the enemy, and it goes to war against them." Joshua looks at Acadia's mom. "Right?"

"Pretty much. Your immune system fights anything in your body that it thinks is trying to hurt you. When you have a cold or get bacteria in a cut, your immune system helps your body recover."

Acadia asks, "So most of the time your immune system is good."

Acadia's mom says, "Actually, it's *very* good. Like your doctor said, it's like your immune system has teams of superheroes going into battle for you. Those superheroes include your white blood cells and your lymph nodes." She touches Acadia's neck. "Some of your lymph nodes are here, by your jaw and ears. Have you ever noticed that this part of your neck gets swollen when you're sick?"

Isabel asks, "How does your immune system help you?"

"If you get a cut and bacteria enter your body, the good cells of your immune system destroy the bad germ cells. If you get a virus, the virus attacks some of your good cells and takes them over, turning them into bad cells. Then those cells reproduce and make more bad cells. Your immune system knows there are invaders in your body, and it destroys the bad cells so they can't keep reproducing."

Acadia asks, "So right now there could be an epic battle happening in my body?"

Acadia's mom nods. "Yes. Your immune system is constantly working hard. We often don't realize how much it does until we get sick."

Joshua jumps in. "I don't get it. With my allergy, my immune system battles against something that it shouldn't fight. Are my superheroes not that smart, or like bullies or something? Why can't they tell the difference between a cold and a nut?"

Acadia's mom pats him on the back. "Your immune system is very smart, and no, your superheroes aren't bullies. Your immune system is working hard to keep you safe."

"It just stinks being different from everyone else," Joshua says while sorting out the candy he can't eat.

Isabel says, "My sister is allergic to pollen, and my mom is *really* allergic to cats. I've always wanted a cat, but we can't get one because of her allergies."

"Don't you get annoyed?" Joshua asks.

"Kind of, but my mom can't help it. She actually really likes cats." Isabel smiles. "Whenever she sees a cat, my mom can't help but pet it. Then she ends up sneezing, and her eyes get all watery. I guess that's her immune system trying to protect her."

Just then, Acadia lets out a loud sneeze. Then one more starts to come out—

"Cover your mouth!" Isabel and Joshua say in unison.

Acadia sneezes into her elbow. "Oh no! What does that mean?"

"Well, you just sneezed out thousands of germs. If it's a cold, let's hope your immune system takes care of it," Acadia's mom says.

"And let's hope our immune systems keep us from getting it," Isabel adds.

Acadia's mom asks, "Do you know the best way to keep from getting a cold?"

"By thanking your immune system for working so hard?" Joshua asks.

Acadia's mom smiles. "Yes. Do you know how you do that? By washing your hands with soap. That's the single biggest thing you can do to prevent germs from spreading. Think about all the germs you probably came in contact with tonight."

"Let's help our superheroes," Isabel says in a singsong voice as she spreads out her bat wings and glides toward the kitchen faucet.

"Then . . . let's feed them!" Acadia says as she eyes her piles of candy.

Acadia's mom shakes her head and smiles as they wash their hands, then happily start eating candy.

The next day, Acadia's mom shows Acadia a special lotion that serves as a model for germs. The lotion glows under an ultraviolet light. You apply it to your hands and go through your day, then use the ultraviolet light to see all the places your "germs" have spread to. Acadia is amazed by how easily germs travel to other locations and people. When Acadia washes the germ lotion off her hands, she gets an idea for an experiment.

MY GERM EXPERIMENT

My Question: How effective is washing your hands with soap at getting rid of germs? Is a quick wash enough, or should you be more thorough?

Research: I researched how washing our hands protects us from germs. I never realized there are two types of soap; regular soap and antibacterial soap. Antibacterial soap kills germs (the bottle claims 99.9%), however some people believe the downside of this is that germs will adapt and become resistant to antibiotics. Regular soap is just as effective, but protects you from germs by lifting them off the skin's surface, then they wash away (so cool!).

Hypothesis: The longer you wash your hands with regular soap, the more "germs" you will remove.

Procedure:

1. Have your subject (I used my mom) apply glow "germ" lotion to his or her hands.

2. Look at the subject's hands under an ultraviolet light.

3. Take photos of the subject's hands.

4. Have the subject wash his/her hands with soap for 10 seconds.

5. Make sure your subject's hands are dry.

6. Take photos of the subject's hands.

7. Have the subject wash his/her hands with soap for 30 seconds.

8. Make sure your subject's hands are dry.

9. Take photos of the subject's hands.

10. Compare photos.

Materials: Subject, glowing "germ" lotion, UV light, soap, sink, camera.

Observations:

Hand with Germ Lotion Stuff and No Washing	Hand After Washing For 10 Seconds	Hands After Washing For 30 Seconds

Conclusion: The germ lotion serves as a model for germs (it's not really germs), but it shows that washing your hands makes a difference. The experiment showed that washing your hands for 30 seconds with soap is more effective at removing germs than washing for 10 seconds with soap. The pictures don't show it that well, but it was amazing/disgusting how many "germs" were around my mom's wedding ring. The fingertips seemed to be the hardest place to get clean. Sometimes I rush when I wash my hands, but now I'm going to try to wash them for 30 seconds.

stay AWAY germs!!!

NEW SCIENCE WORDS

White blood cells

Protect the body from foreign invaders and infection. They are only about 1% of your blood.

Bone marrow

Deep inside your bone: this is where red and white blood cells are produced. White blood cells only have a lifespan of a few days, so new ones are always being produced.

white blood cells help fight infections

Bone marrow

O_2

platelets help control bleeding

O_2 O_2 O_2

Red blood cells carry oxygen throughout the body

Lymph Nodes

These are connected through lymph vessels. Lymph vessels bring unfiltered fluid (called lymphatic fluid) into the lymph nodes, then the vessels carry the clean fluid away. When you have an infection, this is where a lot of your infection-fighting cells gather!

lymph in

blood vessels

lymph out

Spleen

An organ that filters out damaged or old blood cells.

GET OUT!

Skin

The skin is an organ! It's our immune system's first protective barrier.

Super zoomed up skin cell

Things I
Still Wonder:

- Where in my house are the most germs found?

- What can I do to make my immune system stronger?

- I just got the flu shot; does the flu shot impact my immune system?

Further Exploration

The following websites were helpful to me while writing this book and are likely to remain active and helpful to teachers and learners in the years to come.

Frogs (Chapter 1)

http://www.fun-facts.org.uk/animals/animals-frog.htm

http://www.vernalpools.me/the-frogs-of-maines-vernal-pools/

https://www.aza.org/frogwatch-usa-maine

Pollution (Chapter 1)

http://www.kids-against-pollution.org/

https://kids.niehs.nih.gov/index.htm

Frogs at Environmental Indicators (Chapter 1)

http://frogsaregreen.org/

http://cgee.hamline.edu/frogs/archives/corner1.html

Deciduous and Coniferous Trees (Chapter 2)

http://www.maine.gov/dacf/mfs/projects/fall_foliage/kids/meforest-facts.html

https://www.tcv.org.uk/helpingkidsgrow/fun/name-tree

http://blog.nwf.org/2013/03/tree-time-a-kids-guide-to-tree-facts-and-fun/

Emotions (Chapter 2)

http://kidshealth.org/en/kids/talk-feelings.html

https://kids.frontiersin.org/article/10.3389/frym.2017.00011

Water Cycle (Chapter 3)

https://water.usgs.gov/edu/watercycle-kids-adv.html

https://www.metoffice.gov.uk/learning/weather-for-kids/water-cycle

https://www3.epa.gov/safewater/kids/flash/flash_watercycle.html

Time Zones (Chapter 4)

https://time.is/GMT

https://www.npr.org/templates/story/story.php?storyId=7829863

http://alaska.gov/kids/learn/timezones.htm

Allergies (Chapter 5)

http://kidshealth.org/en/kids/allergies.html

http://pbskids.org/arthur/health/allergy/

Immune System (Chapter 5)

https://kidshealth.org/en/kids/immune.html

http://www.chop.edu/conditions-diseases/all-about-immune-system

"Germs" (Chapter 5)

http://www.pbs.org/video/gross-science-how-far-do-germs-travel/

http://www.discoverwater.org/soap-and-water-science/

Other ACADIA FILES Books

Acadia Greene's year of science adventures begins with *The Acadia Files: Book One, Summer Science*, and the best way to follow her growth as a person and a scientist is to start with that book. The next page shows the Book One table of contents; the page after that shows the cover of Acadia's science notebook, which she begins in the summer;

and the page after that shows Acadia's diagram of the scientific method, which she creates to remind herself how science works.

In *Book Three, Winter Science*, Acadia Greene investigates climate change and how to reduce her carbon footprint. The helium balloons at her eleventh birthday party lead to questions about the weights of gases and neutral buoyancy. Paper airplanes bring discoveries in aerodynamics. Tracks in the snow raise questions of how animals survive the winter. And an afternoon of sledding slides right into an investigation of momentum, acceleration, and friction.

And in *Book Four, Spring Science*, Acadia investigates asteroids, meteors, and the age of the Earth; vernal pools; sprouting plants; and emerging insects and other animals. Science is in full action mode in the spring, and that puts Acadia into full investigation mode!

Contents

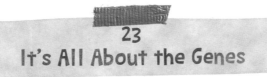

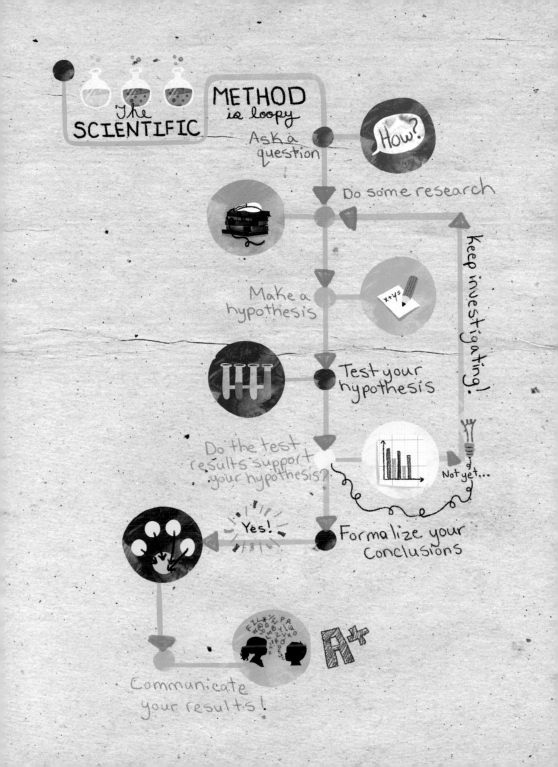

Acknowledgments

A huge thank you to Jonathan Eaton and the staff at Tilbury House Publishers for believing in this project. Thank you to Holly Hatam for capturing Acadia's journal with her beautiful illustrations.

My husband, Andrew, can be seen throughout these stories by those who know him. He gave feedback and ideas from the first draft through the final revisions. Thank you for the support you show me and the support you always give our family.

Thank you to my grown-up beta readers Andrew McCullough, Lindsay Coppens, and Peggy Becksvoort. Each of you brought a unique lens that made the book better. Thank you to my kid beta readers Greta Holmes, Sylvia Holmes, Isabel Carr, Allison Smart, and Greta Niemann for your honest (and very fun to read!) feedback. And thank you to my students at Falmouth Middle School; the sorts of questions you ask were with me as I wrote the stories and created a vision for Acadia's notebook.

And last but certainly not least, thank you to my fact checkers who helped edit and review the accuracy of the scientific content: Andrew McCullough, Grant Tremblay, Elise Tremblay, Sarah Dawson, Eli Wilson, Jean Barbour, and Bernd Heinrich, who generously answered a question no one else could. A lot of minds and a lot of knowledge are behind this book. I couldn't have done it without them.

KATIE COPPENS lives in Maine with her husband and two children. She is an award-winning middle school language arts and science teacher. Much inspiration from this book came from her marriage to a high school biology teacher and from their focus on raising children instilled with compassion, curiosity, and creativity. Katie's publications include a teacher's guide for the National Science Teachers Association, *Creative Writing in Science: Activities That Inspire.* She welcomes you to visit her at *www.katiecoppens.com.*

Children's book illustrator and graphic designer HOLLY HATAM (Whitby, Ontario) loves to combine line drawings, photography, and texture to create illustrations that pack energy and personality. Her picture books include *What Matters* (SONWA children's awards honorable mention), *Dear Girl, Tree Song* and the forthcoming picture book series *Maxine the Maker* (Dial, 2018).

Tilbury House Publishers
12 Starr Street
Thomaston, Maine 04861
800-582-1899 • www.tilburyhouse.com

Hardcover ISBN 978-0-88448-604-6
eBook ISBN 978-0-88448-606-0

First hardcover printing June 2018

15 16 17 18 19 20 XXX 10 9 8 7 6 5 4 3 2 1

Library of Congress Control Number: 2018946460

Cover and interior designed by Holly Hatam and Frame25 Productions
Printed in Korea